Ashley
the Dragon
Fairy

For Isabelle Hudson,
with lots of love and fairy sparkles

Special thanks to Sue Mongredien

ISBN 978-0-545-42595-7

All rights reserved. Published by Scholastic Inc., 557 Broadway, New York, NY 10012, by arrangement with Rainbow Magic Limited.

12 11 10 9 8 7 6   14 15 16/0

Printed in the U.S.A.   40

This edition first printing, February 2012

Ashley the Dragon Fairy

by Daisy Meadows

SCHOLASTIC INC.

New York   Toronto   London   Auckland
Sydney   Mexico City   New Delhi   Hong Kong

The Fairyland Palace

Barn

Farmhouse

Stables

Clubhouse

CAMP

Adventure Lake

Birdwatching Tower

There are seven special animals,
Who live in Fairyland.
They use their magic powers
To help others where they can.

A dragon, black cat, phoenix,
A seahorse, and snow swan, too,
A unicorn and ice bear —
I know just what to do.

I'll lock them in my castle
And never let them out.
The world will turn more miserable,
Of that, I have no doubt!

Contents

The Adventure Begins!

"Bye, Mom! Bye, Dad!" Kirsty Tate yelled, waving as her parents' car pulled away.

Her mom, who was in the passenger seat, rolled down the window. "See you next week," she called. "Have a great time, girls!"

Kirsty grinned at her best friend, Rachel Walker. "We will!" both girls said together. A whole week away at an outdoor adventure camp — it was going to be just perfect!

"Hi, guys," came a voice from behind them. They turned to see a tall, smiling girl with long brown hair. Her red T-shirt had ADVENTURE CAMP COUNSELOR printed on it in yellow letters. "You must be Kirsty and Rachel," she said. "I'm Lucy, one of your camp counselors. I'll take you to your cabin, OK?"

Kirsty and Rachel followed Lucy along a path, feeling very excited. They passed through a small wooded area where Rachel spotted a squirrel bounding up one of the pine trees.

Then they headed out to a sunny
meadow with rolling hills beyond it.
There were wooden cabins scattered
around, each with colorful curtains in
the windows, and front doors painted
in bright hues. Music rang out from
some of the cabins, and Kirsty and
Rachel could see clusters of campers
having fun. There was a basketball
hoop attached to one of the trees and
some boys were playing a pickup game.
A couple of girls were skateboarding
outside another cabin, while
a small group sat at a picnic
table, laughing and
chatting.

   "Here we are," Lucy
announced as she
stopped at a cabin

on the right. It had a light blue door and
blue-checked curtains in the windows.
"I'll let you unpack. After
that, you might want to
explore the camp.
There are maps
everywhere, so you
won't get lost.
We'll all be going
on a cave trip
in about an hour,
OK?"

Kirsty and Rachel
thanked Lucy, then
entered the cabin
feeling curious and
excited about their home for the next
week. There was a bunk bed and four
single beds, a separate bathroom, and

a bulletin board on the wall. Rachel plopped down on the lower bunk and Kirsty threw her cardigan on the top bunk to claim it. "Wow, look at this," Kirsty said, reading the schedule for the week. "Canoeing, horseback-riding, swimming . . . there's so much to do here!" "I can't wait to meet our bunkmates," Rachel said, smiling. "And you never know—we might even make some new fairy friends while we're here, too!"

Kirsty smiled at the thought. She and

Rachel were good friends with the fairies, and they'd had lots of adventures with them. Magical things just seemed to happen whenever the two girls got together! "Come on, let's explore," she suggested. "We can unpack later. I can't wait to look around!"

Rachel agreed, so the girls left their bags and headed out into the sunshine again.

There was a big building in the center of the camp with a sign above the double doors that

read CLUBHOUSE. Close by was a large,
wooden sign with posters behind a
glass case. One was a map with arrows
pointing in different directions—to the
Mess Hall, the sports fields, an outdoor
amphitheater, and more.

"Look, here's a map," Rachel said,
pointing to the colorful sign in
the glass case. She and Kirsty walked
over to it.

"Ooh, a waterfall," Kirsty said, pointing it out to Rachel on the map.

"And there are the stables," Rachel noticed. She blinked. The sun was shining very brightly. As it reflected off of the glass case, it seemed to sparkle. Rachel shielded her eyes. The light was dazzling!

Kirsty was covering her eyes, too.
"The sun is so strong," she said. "I wish
I had my sunglasses!"

Rachel was about to reply when she
heard another voice. "Kirsty! Rachel!
This is King Oberon. The fairies need
your help. Please use your magic lockets
to come to Fairyland as soon as you
can!"

Rachel gasped. So
the glass case really
was sparkling with
fairy magic! Rachel
grabbed Kirsty's
hand and pulled
her to the side of
the clubhouse,
where nobody
could see them.

"Come on," she said, fiddling with the latch of the special locket she always wore around her neck. "Oh, I hope the fairies are all right!"

Kirsty was busy with her own locket. Inside was some magic fairy dust, given to them by the fairy queen herself. Each girl took a pinch and sprinkled it over herself. Then the two held hands as a magical, sparkly whirlwind spun around them. Another fairy adventure had begun!

Off to Fairyland!

Moments later, the girls felt themselves being gently set down, and the whirlwind spun away. They blinked and looked around. "The Fairyland Palace!" Kirsty cried in delight, seeing it in front of them.

"And there are Queen Titania and King Oberon," Rachel realized. "Come on!"

The two friends ran over to the fairy king and queen, who were standing with a group of fairies that the girls didn't recognize. As in the past, Rachel and Kirsty had shrunk to fairy-size now that they were in Fairyland.

"Hello again, Kirsty and Rachel," King Oberon said. Kirsty noticed that he didn't seem as cheerful as usual, and she wondered why. "We've called you here because Jack Frost is up to his tricks again. This time he's really gone too far! He's stolen seven magical animals from our fairies—a dragon, a black cat, a phoenix, a seahorse, a snow swan,

a unicorn, and an ice bear."

"Why?" Rachel asked. "Why does he want them?"

Queen Titania joined the conversation. "These are our Magical Animal Fairies," she said, pointing to the group of seven fairies who stood with her. "Every spring, they get seven new young magical animals to look after and train

for one year. Each magical animal has special qualities and helps spread the kind of magic that every human and fairy can possess—the magic of imagination, luck, humor, friendship, compassion, healing, and courage. The fairies spend a whole year teaching the baby animals how to use and control their powers."

Kirsty still didn't quite understand. She was about to ask a question when one of the Magical Animal Fairies stepped forward and smiled. She had an afro and had wrapped a stylish scarf around her head. Her cargo pants were embroidered with a dragon on one leg, and she wore a striped tank top. "Hi," she said. "I'm Ashley the Dragon Fairy, and this is Lara the Black Cat Fairy,

Erin the Phoenix Fairy, Rihanna the
Scahorse Fairy, Sophia the Snow Swan
Fairy, Leona the Unicorn Fairy, and
Caitlin the Ice Bear Fairy."

Rachel and Kirsty smiled at the seven
friendly faces before them. "Hi," Rachel
said, curious to know more about
these fairies and their animals.

"Each of the magical animals looks
after a different magical power,"
Ashley went on. "The baby dragon

is responsible for imagination. The black cat looks after luck, the phoenix's magical quality is humor, and the seahorse is responsible for friendship. The snow swan inspires compassion, the baby unicorn has the power of healing, and the ice bear looks after the power of courage."

"We spend a whole year teaching the baby animals how to use and control their magical powers," Lara added. "Once the magical animals are all trained, they go back to their families in Fairyland. There, they help spread their magic gifts throughout the fairy and human worlds."

"But Jack Frost kidnapped the magical animals because he didn't want them to be fully trained," the queen explained. "And if the animals aren't trained, they can't help spread their magic, like imagination and humor—qualities that everyone needs!"

"We believe that Jack Frost would like the world to be as miserable as he is," the king added. "He doesn't want people or fairies to have friendship and luck."

Kirsty and Rachel exchanged horrified glances. They couldn't imagine how awful life would be without friendship! And the idea of a world without any humor or courage was too sad for words.

"We'll help," Kirsty said right away. "We'll go to Jack Frost's castle now and get the animals back for you!"

The king smiled. "Thank you, Kirsty," he said. "We knew we could count on you and Rachel. However, something remarkable has happened. Come to the Seeing Pool and we can show you."

The king and queen led the girls and the Magical Animal Fairies to a large blue pool in the palace

gardens. The queen touched the surface
of the water with her wand, and it
shimmered with all the colors
of the rainbow.
A picture started to form on the
water—a picture of Jack Frost
surrounded by all the
magical animals
outside of his
Ice Castle.
Rachel giggled
when she saw
flames blast out
of the little dragon's
nose as he sneezed.
The flames melted
part of the castle's icy
wall! "Oh, no," she said.
"I don't think Jack Frost will be

very happy about that."

"Look at the ice bear!" Kirsty said, pointing to a different area of the picture. A cute white bear was chasing Jack Frost's goblins and freezing them into icy statues with a light tap of its paws.

The girls watched the scene develop into chaos. The magical animals were now happily chasing one another around the castle, completely ignoring Jack Frost's orders. And then, suddenly, a sparkling window opened up in one of the castle walls, and the seven

young animals jumped through it, one after the other.

"Where did they go?" Rachel asked, puzzled.

"Into the human world, it seems," the queen told her. "And there's Jack Frost sending his goblins through the same window, to track them down!"

The girls watched as a group of the goblins scrambled through the magical window and vanished from sight. The window gradually faded away.

"What happened next?" Kirsty asked.

Ashley shrugged unhappily. "We don't know," she said. "The animals must be hiding somewhere in the human world."

"We've got to find them before anyone else does," Erin added. "They're so young, they can't control their magic

abilities—and
they may be
causing
strange things
to happen in
the human
world!"

"We'll help you find them," Rachel said confidently.

"Thank you," said King Oberon. "But you must be careful. As Erin said, the animals aren't able to work their magic very well yet. This might mean that their magic qualities of imagination, luck, humor, friendship, compassion, healing, and courage are more powerful than usual. It might even mean that their special magic does the opposite of what they want it to do, especially if

the animals are nervous."

"The magic qualities will affect anyone who comes near the animals," the queen said. "So watch out for anybody acting strangely—it may lead you to one of them."

"I'll go to the human world with you to search for Sizzle, the baby dragon," Ashley said. "He has a cold right now. He must have caught it while

he was at Jack Frost's Ice Castle. I'm worried about him!"

"You must be careful and stay out of sight," the queen reminded her. "No one

in the human world can know about
Fairyland or anyone who lives here.
Good luck!"

With those words, she pointed her
wand at Ashley, Kirsty, and Rachel.
The three of them had just enough

time to call good-bye. Then another glittery whirlwind whisked them up and took them spinning through the air. . . .

Into the Labyrinth

With a last flurry of sparkles, the
girls found themselves back to their
normal size, and on the campgrounds
once again. Ashley eagerly glanced
from side to side, but then a look of
disappointment crossed her face. Her
glittery wings drooped. "We Magical
Animal Fairies can always tell when our
creatures are nearby," she said, "but I
can't sense anything here."

She was about to say something else when they heard voices. Not wanting to be seen, Ashley darted onto Kirsty's shoulder and hid behind her hair.

"I guess we'd better go back to our cabin," Rachel said. "It must be time to go on the cave trip."

"Keep a lookout for dragons," Kirsty whispered excitedly, as they headed off. Oh, it was wonderful to be starting a new fairy adventure!

Back at their cabin, they saw that

their bunkmates had arrived and were
all unpacking. "Hi," said a blonde
girl wearing a pink baseball cap. "I'm
Emma, and this is Katie, Natasha,
and Catherine."

"I'm Rachel and
this is Kirsty,"
Rachel replied.

"Hi," Kirsty
said to all of them.
She could feel
Ashley still tucked
under her hair. She
hoped that none of
the other girls spotted the little fairy!

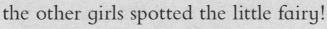

Just then, Lucy popped her head
around the door. "Hi, everyone,
it's time for our trip," she said. "We're
going to the Labyrinth—some hidden

caves deep in the mountain.
It'll be cold in there,
so make sure
you wear
warm clothes
under your
raincoats, and
thick socks
with your
hiking boots. Oh, and
bring some gloves, just in case!"

The six girls quickly got ready. While
everyone was busy, Ashley slipped out of
her hiding place and tucked herself into
the front pocket of Rachel's coat.

"Hey, what's that?" Natasha asked
just then. Rachel's heart almost stopped,
thinking the other girl must have spotted
Ashley. But Natasha was pointing

at Rachel's bed. With a huge rush of relief, Rachel realized that Natasha was talking about a magazine that had fallen out of her bag.

"Oh, it's a new magazine," Rachel replied. "You can borrow it, if you want."

"Thanks," Natasha said, looking happy. "Are we all ready? Then let's go to the Labyrinth!"

The six girls headed out to meet the rest of the campers.

Lucy and some of the other camp

counselors handed out helmets with lights fixed to the front. The counselors led the campers through the campsite.

After a short walk, they arrived at the caves. "I need to do a quick head count to make sure we've got everyone," Lucy said as they gathered at the entrance. She walked around, counting under her breath. "Nineteen, twenty, twenty-one . . ." She frowned. "That's weird.

We should only have eighteen people here. Did I count wrong?"

She swung a large red backpack off her shoulders and rummaged through it, pulling out a roster. "I'll call out the names, then we can see who all is here," she decided. "Emily Adams?"

As Lucy went down the roster, Kirsty noticed a group of campers sneaking off into the cave! "Rachel," she whispered. "Look!"

Rachel's eyes widened. "I'm sure I saw a flash of green," she whispered. "They must be goblins!"

Ashley peeked over the top of Rachel's pocket to see. "Why are they going into

the cave?" she wondered in her tiny
voice.

"Kirsty Tate?" Lucy called out.

"Here!" Kirsty replied.

"And Rachel Walker," Lucy said.

"Here," Rachel said.

"Is there anyone else?" Lucy asked.
She looked relieved when no one
answered. "OK—then everyone's here,"
she said. "I must have counted some of
you twice. That was silly of me. Let's go
into the Labyrinth!"

The group went into the mountainside,

walking through a rocky tunnel that led
into a huge, high cavern.
It was very eerie. Their
voices echoed against
the cave walls, and
they could hear
water dripping in
the distance.
"These are
limestone
caves," one of
the counselors
told the group,
shining her
flashlight up
to the roof of
the cavern. "Up
there are what're
called stalactites—do you see? They

look a lot like rock icicles."

"And if you think they're impressive, wait until we get to the maze," another counselor added. "There is tunnel after tunnel after tunnel. Just as you start to feel really lost, you come out into this magnificent cave full of the most enormous stalactites you've ever seen!"

Meanwhile, Lucy unzipped her jacket. "It's warm in here," she said in surprise. "Usually it's much cooler than this. And wetter, too — but the path isn't slippery

at all today. I'm even going to take my
gloves off!"

Rachel looked down and saw that Lucy
was right. The rocky ground beneath
their feet looked bone dry, except . . .

She frowned and bent lower to take a
closer look. There, on the ground,
was a set of tiny, clawed
footprints—and they
were shimmering
with magic!

"Kirsty, Ashley,"
she hissed, her voice
trembling with
excitement.
"Look—I think
the baby dragon
might have come
this way!"

Searching for Sizzle

Ashley's face lit up with a grin. "That is definitely a dragon's trail. Sizzle must have been here!" she whispered. "And that explains why the cave is so warm. Dragons give off lots of heat, especially if they have a cold and keep sneezing flames!"

"So that's why the goblins are here," Kirsty figured. "They must be looking for Sizzle. I hope they haven't found him yet."

"Can you all get into small groups, please?" Lucy called just then. "We're going to have a race, and the first team to reach the center of the Labyrinth wins. Watch out for the bumpy ground, and no running! Ready, set . . . go!"

The campers all headed off into the maze of tunnels. Rachel and Kirsty struck out alone with Ashley, who flew out of her hiding place to flutter alongside them. If Sizzle was somewhere in the caves, they had to get to the dragon before the goblins or any of the campers found him!

"Oh!" Rachel gasped suddenly. She

stopped and pointed. On the wall ahead, they could see the shadow of a goblin! They could make out his big nose and the bill of the safety helmet he wore on his head. "He must be just around the corner," Rachel whispered, feeling her heart beat a little faster.

Rachel, Kirsty, and Ashley moved toward the shadow. But the goblin must have heard the girls' footsteps because he began running, managing to stay just out of their reach as he thudded through the tunnels.

As they went by, Kirsty noticed a series of black marks on the walls. "These are strange," she said as she ran a finger along one of them. It came away black with soot.

"They must be scorch marks from Sizzle's sneezes," Ashley guessed. "We're getting closer to him!" The girls could hear the voices of the other campers coming from some of the nearby tunnels. Then, as they turned around a corner, they bumped right into a group of three goblins—and they all fell over at once!

Kirsty and Rachel scrambled to their

feet, and so did the goblins. Ashley perched on Kirsty's shoulder, looking worried.

The goblins seemed nervous about something. "It's only some silly girls," one of them muttered, his face a paler shade of green than normal. "Nothing scary."

Another goblin scowled. "I wasn't scared," he mumbled. "Anyway, come on, we've got work to do. We're on a dragon hunt! And we're going to catch it before any of those interfering fairies do!"

The Pogwurzel Plan

Rachel and Kirsty exchanged anxious glances, both thinking frantically. They had to figure out a way to keep the goblins from getting to Sizzle!

Luckily, a great idea popped into Rachel's head. She winked at Kirsty, hoping her friend would play along with her. "You should be careful," she said meaningfully. She spoke directly to the goblin who looked pale and nervous. "Because there are a lot of Pogwurzels in these caves, you know."

The goblins stared. "Pogwurzels?" they echoed, their eyes dark with fear.

Rachel and Kirsty both knew that there were no such creatures as Pogwurzels. But they also knew that goblin mothers often told goblin children that if they didn't behave, a Pogwurzel would come and get them. A lot

of younger goblins still believed in Pogwurzels—and were very scared of them!

Kirsty hid a smile as she joined the conversation. "Didn't you know?" she asked the goblins. "Pogwurzels love caves. They like being in dark, scary places—especially if there are goblins to chase."

While Kirsty was talking, Rachel asked Ashley in a whisper if she would fly around the corner. "And when you hear me shout the word *Pogwurzel*, make a really scary sound!" she added.

Ashley grinned. "Leave it to me," she whispered back. She slipped away unnoticed.

Then Rachel pretended to gasp in
surprise. "Look—what's that?" she cried
in a frightened voice, pointing behind
the goblins. "I think I just saw one!"

The goblins turned in alarm, clutching
one another and looking very scared.

"There's another!" Kirsty cried,
pointing into a shadowy corner.

"I want my mommy,"
whimpered one of the
goblins, staring
around nervously.
"I want to go home!"
cried another, his
lower lip
trembling.
"There's a
Pogwurzel!"
Rachel yelled

in a loud voice. Right on cue, Ashley
used her magic to create a ferocious-
sounding, dragonlike roar!

"Help!" shrieked the goblins, scattering
from the cave. "Let's get out of here!"

Ashley fluttered back to
the girls, grinning in
delight.

"That worked
splendidly,"
she said. "Great
thinking—what
an imaginative
idea! Now let's
keep searching.
I can sense that
Sizzle is close by, in the center of the
maze."

"Great! What are we waiting for?"

Kirsty said eagerly. "Let's get through this maze as soon as we can!"

Unfortunately, it wasn't quite that easy. The girls kept walking through the tunnels, but found dead end after dead end. The rocky walls all looked so similar, it was difficult for them to get their bearings. After a few minutes, they felt completely lost.

Just as Kirsty was starting to worry, they heard a loud sneeze. "Bless you!" she said automatically, and then smiled. "Hey—do you think that's Sizzle?" But then she frowned. Something strange seemed to be happening to her. It felt as if all her ideas and imagination were draining away. Everything in her mind seemed dull and gray.

Rachel also felt weird. She shook her head. "Something's wrong," she said anxiously. "It's like a light bulb has been switched off in my head. I know we should be thinking about what to do next . . . but my brain isn't working."

"Mine, neither," Kirsty said, clutching the sides of her head. "Why can't we think right? This is horrible!"

Fairy Flying

"I think I know what's happening," Ashley said. "Don't worry—Sizzle is causing this problem. Because he's nervous, his powers are working the opposite of how they should, so your imagination is temporarily disappearing."

Almost as soon as she'd finished speaking, all that changed. Suddenly,

ideas were pouring into the girls' heads,
almost faster than they could think.

"Hey—I know what we could do!"
Kirsty said, smiling.

"Oh, yes—I just
had a great idea
for helping Sizzle,
too," Rachel said
excitedly.

Ashley chuckled.
"It looks as if Sizzle's
magic powers are working properly
again, and boosting your imagination!"
she said.

It wasn't just Kirsty and Rachel who
were full of ideas. In the tunnels all
around them, they could hear other
campers talking excitedly. "I just
thought of an awesome story about

being here in the cave," a girl in the
next tunnel said.

"A song about a funny cave monster
just popped into my head," cried a boy
in delight.

"You could make up a cool ghost story
set in these caves," a third person said.

"Everyone's getting closer to Sizzle
and the center of the maze," Kirsty
realized. "We've got to find him quickly,
before anyone else does!"

Ashley nodded. "I'll turn
you into fairies," she
said, waving her wand
over them. "That
way we can all fly
together and
go much more
quickly!"

Green fairy dust swirled around Kirsty and Rachel, and they found themselves shrinking smaller and smaller, until they were the same size as Ashley. They were fairies again! Kirsty fluttered her wings and zoomed into the air. "Hooray!" she cried. "Let's go!"

The three fairy friends flew at top
speed through the maze. All around,
they could hear pounding footsteps
and excited laughter as the other
campers tried to find the middle.

Luckily, the fairies could go much faster than anyone else! Within a few moments they'd reached the center of the maze — and there was a small, green, scaly dragon hovering in midair, with black puffs of smoke coming from his nostrils. "Sizzle!" cried Ashley happily. At the sound of her voice, the dragon's ears perked up. A big smile spread across his face when he saw his fairy friend. Sizzle raced through the air toward Ashley, growing smaller and smaller

as he went. By
the time he
reached
Ashley, he
was so tiny
that he
was able to
leap into her
arms for a cuddle.

"Oh, he's so cute!"
cried Rachel in delight, flying over to
pet him. Kirsty couldn't resist either, and
Sizzle made the funniest little roaring
purrs they had ever heard.

"We've got to be close now," a
voice rang out at that very moment.
"Hurry—I think it's this way!"

The fairies exchanged anxious glances.
The other campers were almost there!

Ashley quickly waved her wand over Kirsty and Rachel, and, with a flood of glittery sparkles, they turned back into girls.

"Thank you so much," Ashley said then. "Now I can take Sizzle back to Fairyland and finish his training. I'd better fly!"

In one last shower of fairy dust, she was gone—just as Lucy emerged from one of the tunnels. "Kirsty, Rachel, good job!" she cried, smiling. "You're the first ones here. No one's ever made it to the center so fast before! How did you find your way so quickly?"

Other boys and girls were now pouring into the central area from the different tunnels around the cave. They were all chatting and laughing happily.

Kirsty and Rachel shared a knowing look. "I guess we just used our imaginations," Kirsty replied.

"It was a lot of fun," Rachel added truthfully. She gave Kirsty a secret smile as Lucy went off to talk to some of the other campers. This

vacation was already off to an exciting start. And with six of the young magical animals left to find, the girls were sure there were plenty more adventures to come!

THE MAGICAL ANIMAL FAIRIES

Ashley the Dragon Fairy has
her magical animal back!
Next, Rachel and Kirsty need to help . . .

Lara
the Black Cat Fairy!

Join their adventure
in this special sneak peek. . . .

North, South, East, West

"Come on, Kirsty." Rachel Walker picked up her backpack and smiled at her best friend, Kirsty Tate. "It's time for our next activity—we're going on an orienteering expedition."

"Oh, great!" Kirsty exclaimed happily, lacing up her hiking boots. "I'm really looking forward to it." Then she grinned. "But, to be honest, I'm not exactly sure what an orienteering expedition is!"

Rachel and the other girls in the cabin — Emma, Natasha, Katie, and Catherine — smiled sweetly at Kirsty.

"Orienteering is when you use a compass and a map to find your way to a meeting place," Emma explained. "All the different teams try to get there first. It's a lot of fun."

"It sounds fantastic," Kirsty agreed.

"I've enjoyed all the camp activities so far," Rachel remarked to Kirsty, as their bunkmates went outside.

Kirsty nodded. "And it's been even *more* exciting since our fairy friends asked us for help!" she whispered.

On the day the girls arrived at the

camp, they discovered that Jack Frost
had been up to his old tricks again in
Fairyland. This time he and his goblins
had kidnapped seven magical animals
from the Magical Animal Fairies.

The magical animals were very rare
because they helped spread the kind of
magic that every human and fairy could
possess — the magic of imagination, luck,
humor, friendship, compassion, healing,
and courage. The fairies trained the
magical animals for a whole year to
make sure the animals knew how to use
their powers. Then they could spread
their wonderful gifts throughout the
human and the fairy worlds.

But Jack Frost was determined to keep
the animals from using their magic gifts.
He wanted everyone to be as grumpy

and miserable as he was! So he and his goblins had stolen the young magical animals and taken them to his Ice Castle. But the animals had managed to escape into the human world, where they were now hiding. Of course, Jack Frost sent his goblins after them, but Rachel and Kirsty were determined to find the young animals first, and return them safely to Fairyland. The girls knew they could count on the Magical Animal Fairies for help.

RAINBOW magic™

There's Magic in Every Series!

The Rainbow Fairies

The Weather Fairies

The Jewel Fairies

The Pet Fairies

The Fun Day Fairies

The Petal Fairies

The Dance Fairies

The Music Fairies

The Sports Fairies

The Party Fairies

The Ocean Fairies

The Night Fairies

The Magical Animal Fairies

Read them all!

■ SCHOLASTIC

HIT entertainment

www.scholastic.com

www.rainbowmagiconline.com

RMFAIRY5

RAINBOW magic™

SPECIAL EDITION

Three Books in Each One—
More Rainbow Magic Fun!